Tides

of

Darkness

Dragon Riders of Osnen Book 13

RICHARD FIERCE

Dragonfire Press

Cover design by germancreative.

Cover art by Nimesh Niyomal

ISBN: 978-1-958354-12-4

CONTENTS

1

I stood on the deck of *The Filthy Jewel* and stared at the unending black water.

A strong wind was blowing in our favor, filling the brown sails and ruffling my hair. I had never been on the open ocean before, and it made me aware of just how small and insignificant I was compared to the vast body of water.

Malin was at the helm, guiding us continually west. Occasionally, he would pull a compass from his sash and hold it up, then he would turn the wheel a bit and nod and mutter to himself before returning the compass to the folds of the red material.

Malin was an interesting man. He didn't bother to wear a shirt, and his skin was tan from the constant sun. When we'd first met, I thought his earrings had merely been solid gold circles, but they were actually coins. He'd drilled a hole in them and wore them in his ears, claiming it protected them from being stolen.

His crew was just as eccentric looking as he was, and I began to suspect they weren't just common sailors. Every one of them bore scars along their bodies, scars that appeared to have been made by swords. Whether Malin commanded a crew of pirates, I didn't bother to ask. It wasn't my business, and as long as he got us to the Whispering Cliffs and back, I had no concern for what he did in his own time.

The galleon shuddered and groaned as it struck a large wave, drawing my focus back to the water. Much to my surprise, I found I enjoyed the smell of the salt ocean and the breeze on my face. I walked to the port side of the ship and leaned over the railing, inhaling a deep breath. I knew nothing about sailing, but it seemed we were moving at a brisk pace.

Another groan, a human one, carried on the air, and I looked to where Maren was. She was sitting cross-legged near the captain's quarters with a bucket in her lap, and a few moments later, she vomited into it. Soon after departing the port, she'd become seasick. She was doing somewhat better now, but she was so exhausted from retching that she could hardly walk.

I felt bad for her, but Malin said he had nothing that would ease her discomfort, so she had to suffer through it. I walked over to where she was and knelt beside her, scrunching my nose at the stench coming from the bucket.

"Can you empty this for me?" she rasped.

"Of course," I replied. I did as she asked and brought the bucket back to her, then sat on the deck next to her.

"Is there any sign of land yet?"

I shook my head. We had been on the ocean for five days now, and there was nothing but black water and blue sky in all directions. I looked up and watched Demris as he soared on the currents, his wings stretched out wide. He and Sion took turns flying with the ship and resting by floating in the water.

"Tyrval never said how far it was," I replied. "Hopefully, we're close."

Maren didn't say anything. She held onto the bucket, her eyes half-closed.

"You didn't get this sick on the ferry. Are you …?"

Maren shook her head slightly. "No, not that."

"Oh." For a moment, I wasn't sure if I was disappointed or not. With everything going on in the world, the last thing we needed to worry about right now was a baby, but still. That fleeting moment of excitement was exhilarating.

"You haven't thought of any spells that will help?"

I had already asked her that, but I was hoping

she might have remembered something. She shook her head again. I rubbed her back comfortingly.

"Go do something," she said. "I don't like you seeing me this way."

I smiled. "You're funny."

"No, I'm hilarious."

At least she still had her sense of humor, despite how she was feeling. I rose to my feet and walked to where Malin was.

"A storm is brewing," he said.

The sky was clear, without a cloud in sight. I gave him an odd look, and he chuckled.

"I can feel it in me bones, boy. It's a strong one, too. When it comes, ye and yer wife should get below. Yer not experienced enough to be out here in the thick o' it."

I didn't disagree with him, so I nodded.

"Since you can sense when a storm is coming, can you also tell when land is near?"

"Afraid I'm not a wizard, so no. If ye could start securing the ship, it'll make me job easier when we come upon the storm."

"Of course."

I went to work tying down everything with rope. The other crew members were doing the same, and I kept looking at the sky to check for clouds. Of course, there were none.

He's right, Sion said. *I can smell the rain coming.*

Are you sure that's not the ocean water in your nose?

I'm sure.

Malin obviously had more experience than me, so I didn't want to question him, but it seemed odd that he could sense a storm that wasn't visible. Perhaps he was magically inclined and simply didn't know it. Then again, he'd been sailing most of his life, so maybe he'd learned to spot things I was missing. I pushed the thoughts away and continued working.

Once all the loose items on the ship were secured, I returned to Malin's side at the helm. His eyes scanned the horizon.

"What is it?" I asked.

"Nothing I can see yet. It's best to avoid a storm when possible, but I don't know which direction she's comin' from. Once I see 'er, we'll need to furl the sails quickly. The wind will tear them to shreds, and without sails, we're dead in the water."

"How do you avoid a storm? It seems it would be too big to escape."

"Speed, me boy. If ye can outrun 'er, ye've guaranteed yerself to live another day. If not, yer fate is up to the sea goddess's mercy."

"You've been in lots of storms?"

Malin nodded. "Aye, too many to count. Even still, it's ne'er a good idea to let your guard down on the ocean. Ye might want to get yer lass below deck now and make 'er comfortable. Once the storm hits, this ship will be as unsteady as me when I've had too much rum."

I was starting to get worried. If a storm immobilized the ship, Sion and Demris could probably pull us to land, but that would delay our journey to the Whispering Cliffs, which in turn would delay our return to the Citadel.

Keep us safe, I prayed, looking to the heavens. I did not aim my word at any deity in particular, just a semi-desperate plea to anyone that was listening. I walked to where Maren sat and helped her to her feet, placing her arm across my shoulder to support her.

"I can't eat anything," Maren said.

"That's not what we're doing," I replied. "Malin says a storm is coming, and he wants you down below in case it gets bad."

"I'm sorry, Eldwin."

"For what?"

"That I'm so weak."

"You're not weak," I said. "You're the strongest person I know. Getting seasick is perfectly normal." I wasn't sure if that was true, but I didn't think a little lie would hurt.

It was a minor struggle to get Maren down the stairs, but once we were below deck, it was easy to get her to our room. She collapsed onto the cot and I set her bucket beside the bed.

"It's right here if you need it. I'm going to get you some broth, and then I'll be back to stay with you. Don't leave this room."

"Where would I go?" Maren asked. "I can barely walk."

I left the room and headed for the galley. Malin had taught me a lot about the lingo used on the ship. The galley was a fancy name for the kitchen. The floor of the galley was lined with tin, which protected the ship from catching fire if hot coals fell from the stove. It was a clever setup, but I was most impressed with the stove. It hung from chains that were attached to the ceiling beams, and it stayed steady no matter how the ship swayed.

Malin had also lectured me on the basic anatomy of the ship. The bow was the front of the ship, while the rear was called the stern. If one were facing the bow, the left side of the ship was called port, and the right was starboard. It was relatively easy to remember the information, though I doubted I would ever use it after this voyage. I stepped into the galley and the cook, Denley, was busy putting the stove's fire out.

"Do you have any warm broth? Maren needs something in her stomach."

"Aye, there's some in the pot there."

The ship's cook had served dinner early, and I was glad to know there was still something left for Maren. I grabbed a wooden bowl and used the ladle in the pot to transfer some of the liquid to the bowl, offering a nod to Denley as I headed back toward my room. I reached the door and was about to open it when the ship lurched. The bowl slipped, spilling some of the broth on the floor, and I cursed under my breath.

A moment later, a bell tolled.

I rushed above deck to see what was happening. In the distance, where there had been clear skies before, dark billowy clouds were visible. I walked to the railing and looked down. The water was choppy, and the waves were steadily growing in size.

"The sails, boy! Help furl the sails!"

I tossed the bowl down and did as Malin commanded.

2

The tempest was upon us.

The fading light of the sun was blotted out by the storm clouds, and we were smothered into obscurity between the black water of the ocean and the darkness above. Lightning arced across the sky, briefly turning night into day. Thunder cracked, and the rain poured heavily from the heavens like a waterfall. Massive waves and powerful gusts tossed both ship and crew about furiously.

Malin was at the helm, fighting desperately to keep the ship's wheel from spinning out of control. He was shouting orders, but I couldn't hear what he was saying. The wind whipped his words away, and the thunder shattered them to pieces. A colossal wave crashed across the deck, sending one of the crew members sprawling. The ship tilted under the barrage of wind and water, and the unlucky person tumbled off the port side into the ocean.

The rest of the crew abandoned their posts and made a mad dash below deck. With the amount of water washing across the ship, I was worried we were going to sink. I fought against the wind and rain to the helm and grabbed onto Malin's arm.

"We need to get below!" I shouted.

Malin cackled like a madman. "Go! I'm in me element, boy!"

He had a rope tied around his waist that

connected to the mainmast, and I realized he intended to remain where he was. If he had a death wish, that was his choice, but I wanted to live. I slid across the deck and hurried below, managing to get into the room with Maren. Her face was pale, more so than before, and I climbed onto the cot and embraced her.

"We'll be fine," I said, though the creaking of the ship made me doubt the vessel would hold up against the storm.

A thunderous boom shook the timber of the ship, and something snapped overhead. Before I could move, a ceiling beam collapsed and struck me in the head. The last thing I saw was Maren's terrified face.

When I awoke, all was quiet. I was looking up at the night sky, and the stars shone bright and clear. I sat up and groaned as everything around me spun, making me dizzy. Bile rose in my throat, and I rolled onto my side and vomited on the sand.

Sand.

We were on land? I wiped my mouth with the back of my hand and glanced around. *The Dirty Jewel* was resting awkwardly against the shore, and a fire burned a few feet away from it. Maren was lying beside me, asleep. Sion and Demris were curled up nearby, and Sion's eyes penetrated the gloom to meet mine.

Are you all right?

My head hurts, I replied. Something was

wrapped tightly around my head, and I reached up to touch it. A bandage.

Maren said something struck you during the storm.

A fragment of the memory came back to me. A ceiling beam broke. I looked at the ship.

What happened?

The storm blew us off course, Sion answered. *Demris saw this island, and we pulled the ship onto the beach.*

I got to my feet and walked on shaky legs to the fire. Malin and his crew were gathered around it, and the captain looked up as I approached.

"Eldwin, yer alive!"

"I've been through worse," I said. "Where are we?"

"I haven't the faintest idea. Never sailed this far west afore. Accordin' to me maps, there ain't supposed to be anythin' here."

"And yet here is an island."

"Indeed," Malin chuckled. "Seems that the maps be wrong."

Doing a quick count of the crew, it seemed we were only missing the one person who fell off the ship during the storm.

"I assume we'll get back to sailing in the morning?"

"That be me hope, but we'll check the ship over

to be sure. For now, we rest and we drink." Malin held up a bottle, offering it to me.

"No thanks," I said. "I'm going to get some rest."

I returned to Maren's side and laid in the sand beside her. Out of instinct, it was tempting to stay up and keep watch, especially since Malin and his crew planned on getting drunk, but Sion and Demris were close enough that I doubted anything would happen without their notice. The ground was uncomfortable, and after much tossing and turning, I eventually found rest.

When dawn came, my headache had subsided. I got up and saw Maren was gone, but Sion and Demris were still curled up nearby.

She's in the trees relieving herself, Sion said.

Thanks.

Malin's crew was sprawled out around the remains of last night's fire, but Malin was gone. I pulled my boots off and walked along the beach, enjoying the feeling of the gritty sand between my toes. I made my way toward the ship, and Malin peered down over the railing at me.

"Bad news," he said.

"What is it?"

"The Jewel here sustained some damage. Nothin' major, but she'll need repairs afore we can sail."

"How long will that take?" I asked.

"A few hours. We should be back on the waves by noon."

We had already lost a full night of travel, but sailing on a damaged ship would only cause more problems. It couldn't be helped. I nodded and walked back up the beach, brushing my feet off and putting my boots back on. Maren still wasn't back, and I was getting worried. I plunged into the tree line, using my sword to hack at the thick undergrowth.

"Maren?"

Ahead and to my right, something rustled in the bushes. I turned my blade tip outward and slowly stalked closer. A flash of movement caught my eye, and then Maren stomped out from behind the bushes. She gave me an indignant look, and I lowered my sword.

"Sorry."

"I found something you should see."

"What is it?"

"I could tell you, but I'd rather you see it. Follow me."

Maren went back into the brush, and I followed her. She moved quickly, as if she hadn't been sick at all the last few days. The deeper into the jungle we got, the hotter and more uncomfortable it became. Sweat gathered on my brow, and it seemed I was continuously wiping it away.

"How far in did you go?" I asked.

"Not too far."

I snorted. It seemed pretty far to me. Glancing back, I couldn't see the beach, only the dense jungle. After a few more minutes of walking, the foliage cleared, and we stepped out onto a worn path. It was overgrown from disuse, but it was clearly man-made.

"This is odd."

"It gets better," Maren said. She grabbed my hand and pulled me along the path. It led to the stone ruins of what appeared to be a building, possibly a fortress. What remained of it was covered with vines and moss, and a darkened doorway led inside.

"What's in there?"

"I don't know. I didn't go inside, but I can sense strong magic emanating from it."

I surveyed the surroundings of the ruins, but it was impossible to tell what sort of architecture had been used. It could have been an old Osnen settlement. I looked at Maren.

"You seem to be feeling better."

"I am. The motion of the ship was unbearable. Now that I'm on solid ground again, I feel fine."

"Good."

A mischievous gleam was in Maren's eyes.

"Do you want to see what's inside?"

"How did I know you were going to ask me that?"

3

The wood of the door had rotted away, leaving only a few pieces still attached to the hinges. I took the lead and stepped through the doorway, stopping short.

"I can't see," I said.

"Here."

Maren spoke a few words and a ball of light formed ahead of me, hovering in the air. It illuminated our surroundings, and I saw the walls were from carved stone just as the exterior was. We were in a long corridor and a familiar symbol was etched on some of the stones. I pointed at it and looked over my shoulder at Maren.

She creased her brow as she stared at it. "What is the Toft crest doing here?"

"That's a good question. Maybe this was a failed settlement?"

"If it is, I've never heard about it. No one has. There's nothing on the maps past the coast, remember?"

"True." I paused. "What if it used to be, but it was removed?"

"It's possible," Maren replied. "It seems odd it would be removed from the maps just because it was abandoned. Unless …"

"Unless what?"

"Unless someone is hiding something."

I looked back down the corridor and stared at the shadows beyond the light's reach. Hopefully, it wasn't anything dangerous.

"I guess we'll find out," I said.

We walked along the hall, which wasn't very tall or wide. If Maren walked beside me, it would be a tight fit. The ceiling was only a foot or so above my head, and the air was heavy and humid. The glowing ball of light moved as we moved, always staying ahead of us. The hall opened into a wide square chamber with a vaulted ceiling. At the other side of the room was a tall wooden door with an iron bar, locking it shut.

Tattered tapestries hanging on the walls depicted epic battles. Some featured armies at war with one another, and others showed dragons flaming cities. Regardless of the scenes, there was one commonality among them: the royal crest.

"This place has to be a failed settlement," I said. "Your family's crest is everywhere."

"I don't understand why all record of it has been erased. My father isn't the type to give up on something like this."

"Judging by the look of things around here, it's been empty since long before your father was king."

Maren walked over to one of the tapestries and studied it closely.

"I think you're right. This is my family's crest, but it's slightly different. It's a version I've never seen anywhere except on the floor of the throne room. That's the oldest chamber in the castle, which means my ancestors are the ones who inscribed it. If this place was built back then, it's hundreds of years old."

"It's built like a fortress, but there's nothing out here. Why would anyone need a castle in the middle of nowhere?" I asked.

"Why indeed?" Maren replied. "Do you hear that?"

We both remained quiet, but I didn't hear anything. "No?"

"It sounds like water."

Maren walked across the chamber to the locked door and stopped. I joined her and together we pulled on the iron bar until it slid to the side. I grabbed the metal ring and pulled the door open. It was a stairwell, but it was flooded. The water level was near the top step, and I could smell the salt. It was ocean water.

"Looks like this is the end of our journey," I said.

"Maybe. Maybe not." Maren sat on the floor and pulled her boots off.

"What are you doing? You're not going down there, are you?"

"Someone built this place for a reason," she

replied. "I think it's worth investigating a little further."

She stood and walked down the first few steps, looking back at me.

"You can stay here if you don't want to go. I'm a big girl."

"I'd rather you didn't go at all, but I know you're going to regardless."

Maren flashed a smile, then dove into the water and disappeared beneath the surface. The glowing ball of light followed her, plunging me into darkness. A brief moment of panic overtook me before I pushed it aside.

What's wrong? Sion asked.

Nothing. I'm fine.

Sion probed my mind momentarily. Satisfied I wasn't in danger, she relented.

Where are you?

Some sort of ruins in the jungle. Maren sensed magic, so we came inside to look around.

Should Demris and I come?

No, you wouldn't fit inside this place. We'll be back shortly. There's not much to see, and the way ahead is full of water.

"Eldwin?"

It was too dark to see anything, but I looked in the direction of Maren's voice.

"I hear you!"

"The stairwell is flooded, but there's a room on the other side that isn't. It's not far. Do you want to come over here?"

"Yeah, I'm coming."

I heaved a sigh and removed my boots, fumbling around in the darkness, then descended the stairs until the water reached my chest. I inhaled a deep breath and dove, swimming blindly until the light of Maren's globe lit up the water. The stairs formed a V shape, and I saw rubble at the bottom that blocked an archway. I continued to the other side and reached the stairs, breaking the water's surface.

Maren was standing at the top, water dripping from her clothes onto the smooth stone floor of another hallway.

"It looks like something collapsed down there," I said. "That's probably why it's flooded."

"I saw that, too. Look, there's another door."

I looked past her and saw a door similar to the one we'd opened to get down here. Or up here. Or wherever we were. I climbed the steps and left the water behind, my bare feet slapping against the floor. We walked together to the door, and I put my hands on it to push it open.

"Wait," Maren said. "The magic is in there. We should be careful, just in case."

I hesitated, my imagination running wild. What

if the room was warded and when we opened the door, we were killed in some horrible fashion? Before I could stop her, Maren lifted her leg and kicked the door open. It flung inward and crashed against the wall, splintering to pieces. I looked at Maren and she shrugged.

"Sorry."

"Is it safe to enter?"

She closed her eyes. A few seconds later, she nodded.

"Yes, it's safe."

I stepped into the room and looked around. It was unlike anything I'd ever seen before. The floor was polished so smoothly that it was like a giant mirror, reflecting the ceiling above. The walls were equally polished, but they were black as night. Suspended in the center of the ceiling was an elegant chandelier. It glowed brightly, but there was no flicker of flames.

The floor was cold, abnormally so. This room also had tapestries on the walls, but these were in pristine condition. Maren entered the room and strode past me toward an enormous chair that reminded me of the throne in the palace. She stopped in front of it, searching for something.

"I found it," Maren said. She stepped behind the chair and returned with a chest. She set it on the chair and carefully opened the lid. I walked over and looked inside. Arranged on a purple velvet material were three crystal orbs. There were impressions in the material for two more, but they appeared to be missing.

"What are they?" I asked.

"I'm not sure, but they pulse with old magic."

Each orb swirled with a different color inside. One was red, one was green, and the third was blue. They were mesmerizing, and I reached out to touch the red one.

"Don't," Maren said, slapping my hand away. "We don't know what they do, and it's not a good idea to mess with unknown magic."

"Right. Well, we found what you sensed, but if it isn't safe to take them, then we should leave them here and get back to the ship."

"I'm not leaving them here. They might be of use somehow."

"How do you expect to get them across the way? That chest is too heavy to carry under water."

"We'll wrap them in that," she said, nodding to one of the tapestries.

I yanked it off the wall and laid it on the floor, and Maren set the chest on top of it, tilting the chest at an angle until the orbs rolled onto the tapestry. She pulled the corners of the fabric together and tied them into knots, securing the orbs. A muffled *clink* sounded as she walked out of the room. I took one last look around and followed after her.

<h1 style="text-align:center">4</h1>

We left the ruins behind and trekked through the jungle back to the ship. Malin and his crew were busy repairing the damage from the storm, and Sion and Demris were still lying in the sand, basking under the bright sun. They both looked up at Maren as she approached.

What did you find? Sion asked.

Some sort of crystal orbs.

Their presence is intoxicating. The magic beckons to me.

Maren stopped short and looked at me.

"Demris says the magic of these things is affecting him."

"So does Sion," I said.

"I'll put them on the ship."

Maren walked down the beach and paused to speak with Malin before balancing on the gangplank to get on the ship. My clothes were still wet, and I decided some time in the saddle would help dry them.

Are you up for taking a short flight? We can scout ahead while we wait on the ship to be repaired.

Being in the air is better than being on the ground, Sion replied. *I grow tired of eating fish to restore my strength.*

I didn't see any animals while we were in the jungle, but maybe your presence has scared them into hiding.

Neither Demris nor I smell any animals here. This island is too small to have anything worth eating, even if there were. I will continue to eat fish, but when we return to Osnen, I never want to see another one.

I don't blame you. Let me tell Maren what we're doing and I'll be back.

I trudged along the beach, and Malin waved at me.

"How long before she's ready to get back out there?" I asked.

"Repairs are almost done. We'll be sailing afore nightfall. Did ye see any fruit while ye were in there? It never be a bad way to add to our stores when we can."

"I don't know if they're edible, but I saw some odd things growing in some of the trees."

"Aye, might be coconuts or bananas. Ye and Maren can gather some and put 'em below deck."

"Will do," I replied. "My dragon and I are going to fly out and see if there's any other land ahead first."

"That's a fine plan, me boy."

I hurried up the gangplank onto the ship, then went below deck to our cabin. I opened the door and Maren looked up, startled. She had the tapestry untied and the crystal orbs were in plain sight.

"What are you doing?" I asked, quickly closing the door behind me.

"I was just looking at them," she replied. "They're so strange. I've never seen anything like them before."

"I don't like that they are bothering Sion and Demris."

"That is curious. Dragons can sense the magic in enchanted items, but it rarely affects them. I want to experiment with these things to see if I can figure out what they do."

"Is that a good idea?"

"How else will we learn about them?"

That was a fair point, but still.

"What if you're messing with them once we're back at sea and the magic does something destructive? We can't make it to the Whispering Cliffs if the ship sinks … or something worse happens."

"I won't touch them while we're sailing," Maren said.

"Then you don't have long. Malin said the repairs are almost finished and then we'll be back out there. He also asked if we could collect some fruit from the jungle."

"Would you mind doing that without me?"

I looked from her to the orbs. Maren was an accomplished sorcerer, so I shouldn't be concerned about her handling them, but I was.

"I know that look," Maren said. "Don't worry about me."

"I'll try not to," I said, leaning in close to kiss her.

I left the cabin and returned to the beach, marching across the sand to where Sion was.

Let's see if there's anything out there, I said. *It feels like ages since we've flown together.*

It hasn't been a week, Sion replied.

That doesn't mean it doesn't feel longer.

I climbed up her shoulder and slid into the saddle. Sion launched into the air, whipping the sand into a frenzy. It didn't bother Demris, but Malin and his crew huddled together to shield their faces. Sion gained altitude and turned west. I saw a couple of islands, but they were smaller than the one *The Dirty Jewel* was on. There were no animals or trees on them, nor was there any remnant of ruins as there were on the other island.

We flew for a few miles before turning around. As far as I could see, there was nothing but black water. We'd been sailing without stopping for five days now, and there was no sign of any land, especially not towering cliffs. Sion landed on the beach further from the ship to avoid blasting the crew with sand again. I dismounted and felt along my clothes. They were mostly dry. It would do.

I trudged into the jungle and began looking for trees that were growing anything that resembled fruit. As I was looking up one tree, I spotted a large green spherical shape, but it was growing near the top of the tree. I estimated the height to be at least fifty feet, and I doubted I could climb that high and cut the thing down.

Would you mind shaking some of these trees? I asked Sion.

A moment later, her bulky form came trudging into the jungle, breaking smaller trees and scraping the bark off others with her scales. She placed her clawed foreleg against the tree I was near and gave it a small push. The spherical thing dropped, and I leaped toward Sion, tumbling at her leg to avoid being struck.

It's not a good idea to stand under the tree when I shake it.

You think?

I rolled my eyes at her and got back on my feet. Surprisingly, the green fruit didn't break open when it hit the ground. I picked it up and found it was heavy for its size. A few others had fallen, too, and I collected as many as I could in my arms and carried them to the ship.

"What are these?" I asked Malin as I stopped at the gangplank.

"Those be coconuts. Hard shells, but tasty insides."

"There's plenty of them in there," I said,

nodding toward the jungle.

"Get as many as ye can."

I balanced up the gangplank and delivered the coconuts to the galley, then headed back into the jungle. I had a feeling this was going to take a while.

5

By the time the ship's repairs were completed, I was exhausted. My arms were sore from carrying coconuts, and I was covered in sweat and grime. I rinsed myself in the ocean and boarded the ship, staying on deck in the sun until I was dry again. I was about to check on Maren when Malin called for me.

I strode to the helm. "Captain?"

"Yer dragons beached the *Jewel*. Can they push 'er back into the water?"

"That shouldn't be a problem," I said.

"Good. Tell 'em to be gentle with 'er."

Can you and Demris push the ship into deeper water? I asked Sion. *But be careful. It seems a bit fragile.*

Yes, we can move it.

"Are we ready to depart?"

"Aye," Malin said.

"You might want to hold on to something."

"All hands brace yerselves!"

Take us out.

Sion and Demris launched into the air and flew above the ship, keeping their wings clear of the masts and rigging. Using their hind legs, they dug their claws into the ship and flapped their wings, forcing the vessel off the beach and into the water. Malin went to the railing and looked over the side. Once we were about a hundred feet from the shore, Malin raised a hand.

"That's good!"

Demris released the ship first, and Sion continued pulling for a moment, setting the prow of the ship toward the west.

"Drop the sails!"

The crew did as Malin commanded. A breeze was blowing in our favor, and the red sails billowed as they caught the wind. The ship lurched forward, and we were sailing once more. I was glad to be traveling again. With almost a full day lost, and unless something had changed back home, we had a single day left before the king's armies would besiege the Citadel.

I had hoped the cliffs weren't far and we would have been back by now, but I suppose that had been wishful thinking. Reality was a harsh and cruel mistress. It didn't seem my help was needed, so I headed below deck to check on Maren. She was probably already feeling seasick. I pushed the cabin door open and stopped in my tracks.

Maren was frozen in place. She was holding one of the orbs in her right hand, and her eyes were rolled into the back of her head. My heart dropped into my stomach and I lunged forward, attempting to slap the orb from her hand. Searing pain erupted in my fingertips and spread throughout my body, dropping me to my knees. I opened my mouth to cry out for help, but my voice had no strength. Sion's presence filled the bond, pushing the pain back.

With my mind clear, I realized I couldn't touch the blasted thing. I considered grabbing one of the other orbs, but I immediately discounted the idea. Glancing around the room, I searched for anything long enough to push the orb from her hand, but nothing presented itself. I drew my sword and gently placed the tip against Maren's palm, then eased the crystal orb from her grasp. It landed on the tapestry and Maren sucked in a sharp breath.

"War," she mumbled. "War. War!"

I tied the orbs back up in the tapestry and set them on the floor, then climbed onto the bed in front of Maren. Her eyes were no longer in the back of her head, but the whites were now bloodshot.

"Maren, are you all right?"

She looked at me, her entire body trembling. She didn't seem to recognize me at first, but then I saw the recognition in her eyes.

"Eldwin."

I nodded.

"What happened?"

"I … I'm not sure. I saw something happening, but it hasn't happened yet."

"What do you mean?"

"The orb. It showed me the future. I think. I'm

not sure. It's all a confusing mess." She burst into tears and I wrapped my arms around her, hugging her close. She sobbed into my shoulder for a long moment, then drew back and wiped her tears.

"Did that thing hurt you?" I asked.

"No. It showed me the future, or perhaps *a* future. I think it was only a possibility of how things will go, but if we do not get the wild dragons to return with us, everything is lost."

"There is always hope."

"Not always," Maren whispered. "If we fail, my father will destroy the Order. I saw him murder you, Eldwin. His sword was coming for me next."

"It wasn't real," I said. "I'm right here. I'm fine."

Maren nodded, but whatever she had seen in the vision had shaken her up. I hugged her again and she laid down on the cot, staring off until her she fell asleep. The magic must have drained her strength.

What happened? Sion asked. *Demris is feeling weak.*

Maren was messing with the orbs we found. She's fine now. Is Demris all right?

Yes. He's floating in the water to regain his strength.

Let me know if anything changes with him.

I will.

I remained in the cabin with Maren and watched her sleep. She groaned a few times and made jerking movements as though flinching from something. Half an hour later, she awoke.

"We're sailing again, aren't we?" she asked.

I nodded. "Seasick again?"

"A little."

"The bucket is on the floor. Other than that, how do you feel?"

"Tired. That magic is nothing to toy with."

"Do you remember what you saw?"

"Yes. It was terrible, Eldwin. The scariest part of that vision is that I know my father will do all the things I witnessed if he can get away with it. We must stop him."

"We will," I swore. "With or without more dragons."

"There is something else. I could feel Sion's presence."

"I tried to get the orb out of your hand. She helped push the pain away."

"No, before that. When I first held the orb. It felt similar to a bond, but that's impossible. We can only bond with one dragon."

She did not imagine that, Sion said. *I felt it, too.*

"Did you figure out what those things are, or what they do besides show you crazy visions?"

Maren shook her head. "It will take more time with them, but that will have to wait," she added hastily. "I promised I wouldn't use them while we're sailing, and I won't."

"Given what just happened, I don't think you should use them at all."

"Sometimes the only way to learn something is by trying. You are right to fear the magic, as all magic can be dangerous, but it is a tool. I just have to figure out how to use them."

I wanted to argue with her, but I knew it was pointless. She was as stubborn as a dragon, and my time would be better spent knocking my head against the wall than trying to reason with her once she'd made up her mind about something.

"Sion and I scouted ahead, but I didn't see any other land," I said, changing the subject. "If the wind holds up, we should cover a lot of distance by nightfall."

"We have to be getting close to the cliffs," Maren said. "The ocean can't go on forever."

6

It was late in the evening, and I was having trouble sleeping. Maren was slumbering soundly, her soft snoring occasionally becoming so loud I thought she would wake everyone on the ship. That wasn't what kept me from finding rest, though. I gently slid off the cot and left the cabin, heading above deck.

Malin was at the helm and I could see someone in the crow's nest, but otherwise, the deck felt abandoned. I wandered over to where Malin was. He held a bottle in one hand and looked at me, offering a toothy smile.

"Canno' sleep, aye?"

"No," I replied. "Do you ever rest?"

"Bah, I can rest when I'm dead, me boy."

He held out the bottle to me, but I shook my head. "No, thank you."

Malin shrugged and took a swig.

"When did you start sailing?" I asked.

"In the womb," he cackled. "Me mother loved the sea."

"Did your father also share a love of seafaring?"

"I wouldn't know, me boy. He wasn't much the fatherly type."

"I'm sorry."

"Don't be apologizing fer somethin' ye didn't do. Did ye know ye're father?"

"I did," I replied. "He died when I was younger, fighting against the False King."

"Aye, I've heard the stories. A bloody battle, that one."

Malin went silent for a moment as he took another swig. He looked past me and his face stiffened with terror. He drew back from the wheel, his mouth opening just enough to issue a strangled cry. I spun around to see what he was staring at.

Rising above the bulwarks was a long, slimy tentacle. The moon illuminated it plainly, and I watched in horror as a second tentacle rose from the water, followed by a third.

"Sea beast!" Malin screamed. "Sea beast on the port side!"

A bell tolled, shattering the stillness of the night.

Sion?

She didn't respond. Her end of the bond was open, and I realized she was asleep. That meant Demris should be awake, but I looked to the sky and didn't see him. I rushed below deck, pushing past the crew as they went the opposite direction, each one armed. Maren was sitting up in bed when I entered the cabin. I grabbed my sword belt and quickly strapped it on.

"What's happening?" she asked, rubbing the

sleep from her eyes.

"There's a creature in the water," I said hurriedly. "Call for Demris!"

"He's catching fish," she replied, getting off the bed. "He's on his way. What does it look like?"

"I didn't get a good look at it, but it had tenta—"

The rest of my words were drowned out as the ship rocked roughly, the timber groaning. Maren grabbed my hand and pulled me along out of the cabin and up the stairs to the deck. She skidded to a stop, and I looked to where I'd seen the tentacles. Two giant eyes scanned back and forth across the ship. A massive mouth full of dagger-sharp teeth was wide open, slimy drool dripping from its lips.

The creature rose over the railing, its body trunk-like but fleshy and bulbous. It used its tentacles like arms and pulled itself onto the ship, a broad flat tail slapping wetly on the deck. A brave member of the crew rushed forward, stabbing a spear into the creature's side. He screamed as the creature slapped him aside with a tentacle, and his body flew end over end beyond the railing, splashing into the ocean.

"What is that thing?" Maren asked.

"Who cares? We need to kill it." I drew my sword, but I wasn't so quick to rush the beast. "I'll draw its attention, you hit it with a spell."

Maren nodded, and I stepped closer to the creature, keeping a wary eye on its tentacles. The other crew members kept a healthy distance, but despite their obvious fear, they held their ground. At the sight of my movement, the creature's focus turned to me. A tentacle whipped through the air, but I managed to duck before it struck me.

The darkness retreated as a green light erupted from Maren's hand, bathing the ship in its brightness. Three globes flared from her fingertips, hissing as they shot forth and struck the creature. If they affected it at all, I couldn't tell. They disappeared into its corpulence, and the green light faded. The gloom returned, seeming darker than before.

A tentacle came flying at me, and this time, I swung my sword. It cut through the fleshy appendage, severing part of it clean off. The creature shrieked, the sound piercing. I tried to cover my ears, but the beast swatted at me with another tentacle. It struck me across the stomach, knocking me over. I slammed against the deck, the wind forced from my lungs.

Maren rushed to where I lay, her expression a mix of concern and anger. I saw her lips moving, but I couldn't hear anything above the pounding in my head. I managed to get some air back into my lungs and sat up on my elbows. A glowing blue barrier surrounded us, and the creature slammed its tentacles into the barrier. Each time it struck, the barrier flickered and zapped the beast.

It quickly gave up trying to get through the barrier and turned its attention to the crew. I scrambled to my feet, but I wasn't sure how to help them. The creature was powerful, and its many tentacles were hard to avoid. They stretched at least eight feet in length, and Maren's magical attack had done no damage to it.

"Any other spells?" I asked.

"None that are safe to use on a ship. I also don't want to risk hitting the crew."

"Where's Demris?"

Before Maren could answer, water sprayed into the air as an enormous form broke the water's surface and launched into the air. What nameless terror was this? Another, much larger, of the creatures on the deck, or something worse?

The figure swooped up into the air and barrel rolled, sending a shower of water droplets across the deck. The lanterns of the ship didn't emit enough light to see what it was, but I knew as soon as I heard the roar. It was Demris.

He stretched his back legs out wide and came down near the ship, keeping his wings away from the masts and riggings. With hardly any effort, he snatched the sea beast off the deck and ascended over the water before tossing the creature into the air. He opened his jaw and released a torrent of flame, scorching the creature and setting it ablaze. It screeched in agony as it descended, splashing into the ocean a few hundred feet from the ship. It remained floating, some of its flesh still aflame. Sion's groggy voice filled my mind.

What did I miss?

7

We sailed for another two days, and the night of the sea beast attack felt more like a dream than anything else. The crew was down a member, as the man who'd been flung off the ship was never found.

As the time passed, I began to suspect that Maren was wrong. Perhaps the ocean did, in fact, stretch into eternity. It was morning, and Maren was still asleep. I didn't enjoy interrupting her rest considering how sick she was, so I quietly left the cabin and trudged above deck to see if Malin needed my help with anything. He was at the helm as usual, but he wore an expression I hadn't seen before: concern.

"What's wrong?" I asked. "Is a storm coming?"

"No," he replied. "The Jewel is gaining speed."

"That's good, right?"

"Look at the sails, me boy. There's no wind."

I looked. He was right. There was no breeze at all, yet the ship was cutting through the water.

"Is it yer sorcerer wife?"

"No, she's too weak to use her magic. Any other ideas?"

"Only one. Maelstrom."

"What's a maelstrom?" I asked.

"It's a curse is what it is. It'll suck a ship to the bottom o' the sea, leavin' nothin' behind."

"Could it be anything else?"

Malin shrugged. "Could be a strong current, but I dun think so."

Do you see anything out of the ordinary? I asked Sion, looking to the sky at her.

No, but I sense a strange sensation in the air.

Magic?

Yes. It's faint, but growing stronger.

"I think we're getting close to our destination," I said. "The place we seek is called the Whispering Cliffs."

"Ne'er heard o' it," Malin replied.

"There are few who have. Stay on course, please. We should see something soon."

"We have to stay on course, me boy. Without the wind, we're at the mercy o' the sea. Ain't got enough hands to row 'er. An' even if we did, it be mighty hard to fight a current."

I stayed next to Malin and watched the horizon expectantly. Seconds turned to minutes, and still, there was nothing but the dark water of the ocean. The ship continued to gain speed, so much so that it felt like the wind was blowing against us. The sails billowed backward, but it did nothing to slow our pace.

"Furl the sails!" Malin ordered.

The crew rushed to obey, and I decided it would be a good idea to wake Maren. I went below deck and found her sitting up in bed. She looked at me and smiled tiredly.

"Where are we?" she asked.

"Still sailing, but a current is pulling the ship. I think we're getting close to finding the cliffs."

"That's good news. If it takes much longer, I fear the Citadel will be under siege."

"If it isn't already," I said. "Anesko won't give up easily. I'm sure he'll find a way to buy the school some time."

Maren nodded. "I'm thirsty."

I poured some water from a carafe into a wooden cup and handed it to her. She drank the entirety of it and offered it back to me. I placed my palm on her cheek and ran my thumb along her hairline.

"I'm sorry you're seasick."

"It's not your fault," she replied. "With any luck, we'll find the wild dragons and return to Osnen quickly. I wasn't built for the sea, I guess."

"I doubt any of us were."

A bell clanged suddenly, startling me. "What is that?"

"I don't know. We should probably go see."

I helped Maren off the cot and we left the cabin, heading up the stairs to the main deck. The entire crew, except the lone man in the crow's nest ringing the bell, stood at the prow.

"What's going on?" I asked as we joined the others.

Malin turned around, his countenance grim. "We've sailed to the end o' the world."

I didn't know what he was talking about. I released Maren and pushed my way through the crew to the railing of the bow. A few hundred feet ahead, the ocean disappeared, and I could hear the roaring sound that reminded me of a waterfall.

"Please tell me I'm seeing things," I said.

"We all see it," one of the crew members said. "We're heading to the depths!"

I turned to face Malin. "Turn the ship around."

"I can't," he replied. "The current be too strong. If I tried, the force could break the rudder."

"I think that's a risk worth taking, considering the alternative. Don't you?"

The entire crew looked at Malin expectantly.

"Bah! Ye're a fool, me boy. A blasted fool!"

Malin grabbed the wheel and began turning it to the left. His muscles flexed under the strain, and a few of his crew members rushed to assist him. The ship groaned in protest, but it started to change course.

"We're not going to make it," someone muttered, but when I looked to see who spoke, whoever it was didn't reveal themselves.

"Maybe I can use my magic to help," Maren suggested.

"No. You're drained as it is. If Malin can't turn us around, our dragons will have to lift the ship and carry us to safety."

"Where are they?"

I looked up and realized they were nowhere to be seen.

Sion?

The bond was clouded, and my words disappeared into oblivion. I looked at Maren. "Demris?"

She shook her head. "Something is blocking our connection."

"Magic?" I asked, though it wasn't a guess.

"No, I don't sense anyth … wait." She closed her eyes, her brow creasing with her concentration. "Yes. It's almost imperceptible, but there's a ward nearby. It's crafted so well that I almost missed it. Maybe I can—" a sudden cry of pain cut her words off. Maren dropped to her knees before falling to the deck.

"Maren!"

I knelt beside her and brushed the hair from her face.

"Maren."

"I'm all right," she said. "I touched the ward

with my mind and it seared my consciousness." She blinked a few times and pushed herself into a sitting position. "Whoever created the ward did not want to be found."

"The Wild Ones," I whispered, glancing around at the crew.

"I think you're right."

The Dirty Jewel shuddered, knocking several people off their feet. Four men, including Malin, were at the helm, and they were all red-faced, their muscles bulging as they tried to keep the wheel from turning. Timber cracked, and the ship jerked roughly to the right.

"The rudder snapped!" Malin shouted. "We're doomed!"

Sion? Can you hear me? We need your help!

My words disappeared into the gloom just as before, and I still didn't see her in the sky. Was there an illusion masking them from sight?

"Sion!"

Nothing. We were on our own. I helped Maren to her feet.

"Get to the cabin," I said. "You'll be safer in there than out here in the open."

"If we're falling off the edge of the world, it doesn't matter where I go," she replied. "If this is the end, I want to be at your side."

The words stung my heart, but she was right. And if this was the end, I didn't want to be without her, either. I nodded.

"So be it."

I turned to the prow and watched as the ship headed straight for the edge. My instincts told me to close my eyes, but my body stubbornly refused to obey. I watched helplessly, terror drowning out everything else.

Someone grabbed my hand. I looked over my shoulder to see Maren. She had her eyes closed, and her lips were moving, though no sound escaped them. Was she praying? No, she was working her magic. I felt it tingling my flesh. Goosebumps rose on my arms, and I shivered.

The sky changed. It was only a small portion directly behind the ship, but I noticed it. The blue sky and white clouds were distinctly brighter while the rest of the sky was muted. I didn't know what she was trying to accomplish, but whatever it was, it hadn't worked.

The ship tilted and we descended into the abyss.

8

I felt myself slipping off the deck and lunged toward Maren, wrapping my arms around her. The thundering of the water overwhelmed all other sounds, and I was certain the crew was screaming. I held onto Maren as tightly as I could, praying to any god that would listen.

A roar split the air, followed by another. Maren and I crashed hard against the deck of the ship, and from my periphery, I saw a flash of red and green.

Sion!

She roared again, and this one was full of fury. The ship lurched, and I released Maren and rolled onto my back. Sion and Demris had grabbed onto the ship and were carrying it in their claws, but instead of going up, we were going down.

What you are you doing?

Look there, she huffed.

I scrambled to my feet and grabbed onto the railing for balance. Far below us, towering brown cliffs jutted up from crystal clear water. I immediately recognized them from my dreams.

"We made it," I said, turning to look at Maren. "We made it!"

Maren staggered across the deck to where I was and wrapped her hands around my left arm.

"Tyrval was telling the truth," she whispered. "It is an actual place."

To the right of the cliffs was a long beach, and Sion and Demris flew toward it, gently dropping *The Dirty Jewel* on the shore. The ship shuddered briefly as it listed starboard in the sand, then all was still. Malin shakily walked past me, staring up at the cliffs.

"Blast me to the Void," he said softly. He turned his head to look at me. "There *is* land to the west."

Surprising someone like Malin probably wasn't an easy feat. Despite the danger we were in, I couldn't help but smile at his reaction. The wild dragons had not seen humans in many years, and it was likely they would flame us before we had the chance to plead our cause.

I will not let these wild dragons harm you, Sion said.

I appreciate the loyalty, but I'm sure you and Demris are outnumbered. They could slaughter us all if they wanted.

Sion rumbled her displeasure, but she didn't argue. She knew I was right.

"Can you repair the rudder?" I asked Malin.

"Depends if it's still attached. If it not be …" he shrugged. "We'd have to fashion a new one. Wood from those trees should work nicely."

I drew closer to him and lowered my voice. "Whatever you do, don't stray too far from the ship."

Malin raised his brows. "Why not?"

I pointed to the cliffs. "Dangerous creatures live there. If they see you, they may attack. Fix the ship and wait for us to return."

"Where ye going?"

"To speak with the dangerous creatures."

"Ye're crazy, me boy. Come back in one piece, aye? I've grown to like ye."

"I will," I said, hoping I wasn't lying. I considered how he and his crew might escape if the wild dragons killed me and Maren, but they were unlikely to get far before the same fate befell them.

"You ready?" I asked Maren.

"Yes."

The crew positioned the gangplank as best as they could given the awkward angle the ship was sitting at, and Maren and I walked down it to the beach. Sion and Demris were waiting nearby.

"Should we take them?" I asked lowly.

"Why wouldn't we?"

"If our presence hasn't been noticed yet, it will be when two foreign dragons come flying for the caves. We may have the element of surprise if we go without them."

Maren looked past me and shook her head. "How are we going to get up there? Climb?"

"Yes?"

"How about no," Maren replied. "If we could even scale that thing, it would take hours. Sion and Demris can get us up there in no time. The dragons will know we are here one way or the other. I don't think surprising them will be a good thing."

"That's fair," I said.

To be honest, I didn't really want to attempt climbing up the cliff face, but it seemed like the best option for stealth. Maren made a great point. The dragons probably wouldn't be happy to see us at all, but especially so if we snuck up on them.

"We narrowly avoid one death to face another. I'm sensing a pattern."

Maren stifled her laughter. "Indeed. And if we avoid death here, we will face it again when we get back to the Citadel."

There really was nothing funny about it, but it took some of the edge off. I took Maren's hand, and we walked up the beach to where Sion and Demris were. I pulled Maren in for a quick kiss, then we parted and each climbed onto our dragons.

Take us up there, but be vigilant. We don't know what to expect.

Sion launched into the air, the wind from her wings swirling the sand around beneath us. She gained altitude and winged her way toward the front of the cliffs. I looked back and saw Demris close behind us. Cold uncertainty sat in the middle of my stomach like a weight, and I shivered despite the heat.

As we drew nearer, the shadowy cave entrances I'd seen in my dreams became visible. There were too many to count, but I considered that a good thing. Even if only a handful of the wild dragons agreed to come back with us, that would bolster our numbers tremendously. That was assuming they didn't tear us apart.

They are watching us, Sion said.

You can see them?

No, but I feel their eyes on me. They hide in the darkness.

I stared intently at the gloom, wondering if these dragons looked the same as Sion and Demris. Had living in another land without human interference changed them in some way? I could only imagine.

Where should we land?

There, I replied, pushing the image of the cave entrance I was looking at through the bond. *We'll start with that one.*

It looked like the one from my last dream where the wild dragon had pushed me off the ledge. With Sion here, I was confident that wouldn't happen. She adjusted course and flew straight for it. We were less than a hundred feet away when a flash of color streaked out from the cave. A second later, a roar overpowered the wind in my ears.

I whipped my head to the side and looked down, trying to spot the beast, but I didn't see anything.

Where is it?

He's quick, Sion said. She whirled around and I saw him. He was slightly smaller than Sion in length, and he was thin, skinny even. It was an odd sight, but I didn't have time to speculate. The blue dragon was coming directly for us. He roared in challenge, saliva dripping from his jaws. I felt Sion tense, and she slowed her pace.

Brace yourself, she said.

The two dragons collided, and the world around me started spinning.

9

I gripped the saddle and held on with all the strength I could muster, but the force pulling against me was too much. My hands slipped free and I could feel my legs getting ready to go next. The fleeting thought that if I fell I would land in water was only mildly comforting.

The spinning abruptly stopped, and through my dizziness, I could see Demris had joined the fray. Sion drew back and let Demris deal with the dragon.

Are you all right?

I'm fine. Just a little disoriented, I replied.

Once the world stopped turning, I watched Demris toss the blue dragon around like a tiny doll. Demris was bigger than Sion, and he appeared even larger next to the blue dragon. Perhaps he was a juvenile.

He is full grown, Sion said. *Something must have stunted his growth.*

He looks lean. Do you think he's starving?

I don't know. The others are afraid. Their fear fills the air.

The blue dragon broke away and fled, returning to the cave he'd come from. Demris joined Sion, and I looked at Maren to see if she had been injured. She appeared to be fine and nodded at me.

Take me to the cave, please. Perhaps now that he's suffered defeat, he'll be willing to talk.

Sion glided to the cave opening and tucked her wings in at the last moment, landing inside. She used her claws to halt her momentum. The dragon was scuffling around in the darkness, his heaving breaths loud inside the same chamber. I slid out of the saddle and saw Demris wheeling around in the sky.

He's making sure we don't get trapped in here, Sion said.

Good idea.

I tried to walk past Sion, but she kept her bulk in the way and wouldn't let me pass.

What are you doing?

He may look frail, but he can still kill you. Stay behind me.

I conceded the point and stayed where I was.

You there, I said, reaching my mind out to the dragon. He ignored me. I expected as much, but I would not give up that easily.

Are you injured? My friend is a sorcerer and can heal you.

Go away, the dragon's voice was just as feeble as he looked.

Are you the leader here?

You must be mind-deaf. I told you to leave.

I'm not leaving until I get some answers, I said.

You are going to get us punished. Please leave.

Punished? By who?

The dragon rumbled irritably, and I could feel the vibrations through the cave floor.

How did you find this place?

The Assembly told me about it.

What is the Assembly?

They are the council of dragons.

I have never heard of this council. Drakus is the only ruler here. When he finds out you have invaded his territory, he will not show you mercy.

I'm not afraid of him, I said.

You should be.

My dragon says you are frightened. Are you scared because of Drakus?

Everyone fears Drakus.

Is he your king?

The dragon made a sound in his throat that sounded like laughter, but there was no mirth in his chortle.

You must be a human. They have kings. We have no kings here, only the god Drakus. You should go before he finds you here.

I had even more questions now, but I didn't want to waste time. Whoever Drakus was, he sounded like a menace.

I came here for a reason, I said. *We humans are in need of help. Your help. In my land, dragons share a bond with humans and we work together for the good of the land. Without your help, the Order will fall. Will you help us?*

I know nothing about what you speak of, but I cannot help you. Drakus has forbidden us to leave this place, or he will hunt us down and eat us. As you can see, I have little meat on my bones, but that does not mean I want to die.

Where is Drakus?

On the other side of the cliffs. That is where he spends most of his time.

Will he speak with me?

The dragon laughed again, but this time the sound had some humor to it.

He will flame you before you step into his cave. He despises humans.

Why?

He does not speak of such things to us. His past is a mystery, and I prefer to leave it undisturbed. Did you come here only to ask for help?

Yes, I answered.

Then your journey has been for nothing. We do only what Drakus wants, and he will never agree to help you.

Drakus reminds me of the king in my lands. He is a tyrant and thinks he is above everyone else.

They sound one and the same, the dragon said. *I feel for your plight, but we have our own to deal with.*

I stared into the darkness and eventually saw the dragon's eyes glowing faintly. He returned my stare unblinkingly. I laid a hand on Sion.

These dragons are being held prisoner here, I said.

By the wards?

No, by one of their own kind. His name is Drakus. He has a great disdain for humans, apparently. I suspect he may be as old as Nemryth and the other Assembly members, which means he was there when they made the pact with humans. These dragons will do nothing without Drakus's permission.

Then we must persuade Drakus, Sion replied.

I think that will be easier said than done.

If we cannot persuade him, then he must be removed. It does not sound like he cares for these dragons, so perhaps we will do them a favor.

I had the same thought, but it seemed rather dark to consider. If Sion was of the same mind as I was, then perhaps it wasn't wrong. The beginning of a plan started to form in my mind, but I would need Maren on board. I looked over my shoulder at Demris. He continued to guard the sky, slowly flying back and forth. I turned my focus back to the blue dragon.

If Drakus can be convinced to let you help us, will you come?

I doubt you will get an opportunity to speak to Drakus, but tell me, human, why would we want to help you? I have heard nothing good about your kind.

Consider for a moment that everything Drakus has said about my kind is a lie.

Why would our god lie to us?

Why indeed? I asked. *If I had to guess about his intentions, I would say it's about control. He has power over you because you submit yourselves to him. If you knew what the rest of the world was like, I do not think you would stay here. You looked starved. I assume the others look much the same as you do?*

The dragon didn't answer, so I continued.

In my land, dragons are revered. They never go hungry, and they form a bond with humans that cannot be broken. We become as one, sharing our thoughts and desires with one another.

Like a mate?

I considered my feelings toward Sion and Maren.

The bond is deeper than even that, I answered.

Truly?

Yes. Sion here can attest to it.

There was a long pause, and I realized the

dragon was talking to Sion. I waited patiently. Finally, the dragon's voice echoed in my mind.

I believe your words, he said. *Sion has shown me what your land is like, and I must admit that I would be glad to see it.*

Good!

Hold your excitement, human. First, you must convince Drakus.

I did not enjoy hiding the truth, but I knew I could not tell this dragon what I intended to do. I never imagined that one day I would have to kill a dragon.

10

"Do you hear yourself?" Maren asked.

We stood atop the plateau of the cliffs, and Demris and Sion waited nearby.

"I don't feel good about it," I said, "but it is clear to me that this Drakus has made the wild dragons his slaves. They know nothing about the world except what Drakus has told them."

"And Sion is fine with this path?"

"She's the one who suggested it."

Maren flicked her gaze to Sion, then back at me. "First the Carver, and now a dragon? What's next?"

I shook my head. "The situation with the Carver was different. You know that. And so is this."

"Is it?"

"Yes."

"What happens when these dragons find out the truth? What if they turn on us?"

"They won't find out."

"How do you know that, Eldwin?"

I didn't know that for certain, but I was confident. They feared him, so they would never go to his cave to investigate. And once we were back in Osnen, they would have no reason to return to the Whispering Cliffs. The plan was too simple to fail. I said as much, and Maren sighed.

"You know I will follow your lead, whether not I like your idea. For the record, I do not like this."

"Noted," I replied with a smile.

"What's your plan?"

"Drakus is on the other side of the cliffs. We'll sneak inside his cave, and you'll use your magic to hold him still while I use my sword to end his reign of terror."

Maren frowned. "Sounds too easy."

"I know. I'm sure it'll be much more difficult than that, but if things don't go in our favor, we'll flee the cave and our dragons will catch us. Then it'll be four against one."

"I don't like this idea. What if Drakus calls the other dragons to come to his aid?"

That gave me pause. I hadn't even considered that. I cleared my throat.

"We better not fail at taking him out in his cave."

Maren looked to the sky. "Evening will be here soon. Do you want to wait until morning?"

I shook my head. "No. Anesko and the others are waiting for us. I want to get this done now."

"Very well."

We walked over to where Sion and Demris waited.

We're going to enter the cave alone, I said. *Once we're inside, we'll be at a disadvantage, but if we can take Drakus by surprise, then the risk should be minimal.*

If you are killed ... Sion trailed off.

Yes, yes. You'll flame him and everything else.

You know me well.

Wait at the edge of the cliff and be ready in case we have to jump out of the cave.

We will catch you.

I patted the scales on her legs and looked at Maren.

"Ready?"

She nodded.

I'll see you soon, I told Sion.

You better.

Maren and I walked across the plateau to the opposite side, stopping at the edge of the cliff. I looked down and saw only one cave entrance roughly a hundred feet down. It was enormous, and I wondered just how big of a dragon Drakus was. I scaled down the side of the cliff face first, my muscles straining with every movement. When I reached the cave, I was already sweating heavily. I stayed at the entrance and watched Maren as she made her way down.

"Why couldn't we have our dragons bring us down?" she huffed.

"Because Drakus might sense them or hear the flapping of their wings. I'm sure humans have never been here, so I doubt he would be listening for softer sounds."

"I hope you're right."

"If we need to say anything, let's whisper."

"How about we don't talk at all?" Maren replied.

"Good idea."

We stared at one another for a moment, then I nodded at her and headed inside. A few feet into the cave, the air became noticeably cooler. I drew my sword slowly, careful not to make a sound, and continued onward. The darkness surrounded me, and I reached back with my free hand and grabbed onto Maren's.

I stepped quietly, peering into the shadows as I waited for my eyes to adjust to the gloom. The walls of the cave started took shape, and after a few more steps, I stopped. Maren squeezed my hand.

"What is it?" she whispered.

"There's nowhere to go."

"What do you mean?"

I pulled her beside me.

"It's just an empty cave. There's nothing beyond the wall in front of us."

"Maybe it's an illusion. I can sense magic here."

She reached forward and gently laid a hand on

the wall's rocky surface. It looked solid to me.

"The wall is real, but … there's something odd."

"What?" I asked.

"There's a web of spells concentrated in this area. Let me see if I can—"

Before she could finish her sentence, the floor beneath us disappeared and we fell into darkness. My stomach did flips as we dropped, and I couldn't stop the scream that escaped my throat. We crashed against a rock wall, but it was polished smooth and we slid downward as though we were traveling through one of the garbage chutes at the Citadel.

Without warning, the stone leveled out, and we were dumped onto the floor. Glowing moss lined the ceiling, and torchless flames burned along the walls, illuminating a giant open chamber.

"Is this an illusion?" I asked.

"No," Maren answered. "This is real."

I stood up and brushed myself off, then helped Maren to her feet before retrieving my sword, which had landed a few feet away. I looked around the chamber, but I didn't see a dragon anywhere. Where was Drakus?

"I don't see an exit," Maren said.

"There has to be one. Come on, let's see if we can find anything."

We walked across the cavern and rounded a massive boulder to find a makeshift throne. It was made of sticks and bones, and the bones looked to be from dragons. Affixed atop the chair was a sapphire as big as my first. The throne sat in front of a rectangular table crafted of stone. The edges were conchoidal, and the design reminded me of shells I'd once seen. A silver plate held a half-eaten slab of meat which appeared to be rather fresh.

"Someone's here. That, or they left recently," I said.

"This setup doesn't look like a dragon's. If I didn't know any better, I'd say a human lives here."

The sound of rocks clattering nearby startled me, and I pushed Maren behind me and brought my sword up, ready to fight whoever was coming. A bipedal shadow appeared on the wall, growing larger and larger as the body it belonged to approached.

"Get your spells ready," I whispered, looking at Maren over my shoulder. She nodded, her eyes focused ahead.

The shadow disappeared, and a moment later, a man stepped into view. A crown fashioned from bone rested on his head, and he wore a necklace with a sapphire pendant. It looked eerily similar to the ones the Assembly wore. The man was muttering to himself and staring at the ground, but as he got closer, he looked up and halted when he saw us. His lips curled into a devious grin.

"What do we have here?"

11

"Drakus, I presume?"

"It isn't often I find myself surprised, but here I am astounded twice over. Not only are humans in my domain, but they know my name." The man narrowed his eyes at me. "Who are you?"

"That's no concern to you," I replied.

"I like to know the names of my prey," Drakus said. "I remember them all. Putting a name to the face makes it easier, considering how many there have been."

"You won't be eating us, I can assure you of that." I pointed the tip of my blade at him. "Why do you walk around in human form if you hate us so much?"

"I see you've spoken to the dragons who live here."

"Why do you say that?"

"No man lives today who remembers me, and I doubt your history books mention my name. That doesn't explain how you found my domain."

"The Assembly told us about this place."

Drakus frowned. "Ah, it all makes sense now. It seems my brethren haven't forgotten their grudge against me. Did they send you here to kill me? It took them plenty long enough to find the nerve."

"We're not here to kill you," Maren said. "We came here to find help."

Drakus laughed. "Help? Why would you expect to find help here? It is no secret I despise your kind. I will never help you."

"We don't want *your* help," I clarified.

"You want my dragons." Drakus scowled. "I will not allow them to become slaves to humankind. We have lost enough of my brethren to the perversion of the bond. I will suffer it no longer."

"It isn't up to you," I said. "It is up to them."

"You are mistaken, boy. I rule over these dragons like a god. They would stop breathing if I commanded it. I have heard your plea, and I refuse. Your stench has filled my cave long enough."

Drakus reached up and jerked the collar from his neck. For a moment, nothing happened. We stared at one another in silence until Drakus's body began to change. His skin darkened until it was a cobalt tone. He dropped to his hands and knees, and his body wracked with spasms so strong that his arms and legs trembled visibly. His shoulder blades protruded grossly from his back, and I wrinkled my face in disgust.

Bones popped and crunched, and Drakus's shoulder blades elongated and transformed into wings. His body lengthened and grew in size until he towered over us. A long snout took shape from his humanoid face, and his blue flesh morphed into scales. When his transformation was done, Drakus was one of the largest dragons I had ever seen.

Foolish humans, the dragon snarled. *Your end will be swift.*

Drakus inhaled a deep breath, and flames poured out of his jaws. My eyes widened, and I felt the heat wash over me. I expected dragon fire to envelop and scorch me from existence, but the flames parted a few feet in front of me, branching to the sides and fading into nothingness. I didn't have time to question our fortune. Drakus seemed equally confused, and Maren pushed me aside and raised her hand, casting a spell at the beast.

He roared in surprise as an unseen force pushed him down until he was lying on the floor of the cave.

Release me! he demanded.

"I don't think we will," I replied, glancing at Maren. She met my gaze, but there was concern in her eyes. I raised my brow questioningly.

"Hurry," she whispered harshly.

I realized Drakus was fighting against her magic, and she wasn't likely to keep him pinned down for long. I raised my sword and stepped closer.

"Your tyranny is over," I said. I brought the sword down against his head, but my blade bounced off with a clang, the reverberation so powerful it hurt my arm. I dropped the weapon with a gasp.

Drakus's laughter filled my mind. It was a

rather horrifying sound.

Your pathetic weapon cannot harm me. I am a dragon!

"He's breaking free," Maren warned.

Sion, can you hear me?

Where are you? she replied. *This cave is empty.*

The floor is an illusion. We need your help down here.

"Do something!" Maren cried out.

I picked my sword up and jabbed the tip forward, aiming for Drakus's eye. His lid closed, and my blade skid across the protective membrane, flying wide. I could see him straining against the magic.

We're running out of time, I told Sion.

There's nothing here.

Keep looking!

Drakus's body lifted suddenly, and vibrations rang through the air as Maren's spell broke. She started muttering the words to another incantation, but she wasn't fast enough. Drakus lunged at me, his jaws open wide to snap me up. I threw myself to the side, narrowly avoiding his razor-sharp teeth.

His claw slammed down on top of me, his talons easily ripping through the stone floor. He pushed down on me, pinning me in place. A suffocating feeling washed over me and I started to panic. This was probably what it felt like when Maren had trapped him with her spell. I stared up at him, but Drakus wasn't looking at me. His head was snaking toward Maren. I tried to yell a warning, but I didn't have enough breath to utter anything.

A flash of blue light erupted from Maren's hand and formed a sphere around her. Drakus chomped down on the sphere, but it withstood the force of his jaws. He tried vainly a few more times to break through the magic, but it was no use. He rumbled his displeasure and turned his attention back to me.

I will deal with you first. The woman will die next.

Don't you dare touch her, I replied.

Maybe I'll kill her first and force you to watch. That would be satisfying.

You're vile. Dragons are supposed to be noble.

Drakus snorted. *According to who? Dragons are at the top of the food chain. We answer to no one. I tire of this game, but before I flame you, why did the Assembly send you here for help? They must be desperate indeed to come begging for aid.*

Our fates are twined together like rope, I said. *Neither of us will have a future if we don't work together.*

Dragons lived perfectly well without humans for centuries. We'll be fine long after your kind is gone. Did you come here willingly, or did Nemryth force you? She always ruled with iron talons. I admired that about her, but I couldn't stomach the pact she made with humankind.

I glanced at Maren. Her lips were moving again. Another spell.

I came here on my own, I answered. *Though Tyrval is the one who asked me to.*

My sister is behind this? I'm not surprised.

I didn't understand how Tyrval could be his sister since she was a white dragon and he was a blue, but that didn't matter right now. I needed to keep his focus on me until Maren could finish her spell.

I have all I need from you.

Drakus opened his mouth. I could feel the heat radiating from his jaws, despite there being no flames yet. I looked at Maren one last time and mouthed the words, *I love you.*

A flicker of orange drew my eyes to the back of Drakus's throat. I didn't want to watch the flames come for me, but my eyes wouldn't obey my mind and remained open, staring morbidly straight ahead.

"Stop!" Maren screamed.

12

The flames in the back of Drakus's throat sizzled out of existence. He turned his head toward Maren. Had she used her magic to stop him?

"Let him go," Maren pleaded.

To my surprise, Drakus lifted his claw off me. I expected it to be a ruse, but the dragon made no move to stop me as I got to my feet. His gaze remained fixed on Maren, and I had the feeling that something unusual was happening.

"How did you do that?" I asked.

"I don't know. All I did was speak."

I stared at Drakus curiously, but the beast kept its gaze on Maren. We stood there in silence for a long while, and the dragon didn't move at all. I took a step toward Drakus to see what he would do.

Nothing.

I took another step, and another, closing the distance until I was close enough to touch his leg. Hesitantly, I laid a hand on him. He didn't respond. It was almost as if he was in some sort of trance. I retreated to Maren's side and pointed at the ground.

"Lie down."

Again, nothing. I frowned and looked at Maren.

"You try it."

"Try what?" she asked.

"Try telling him to do something. I think you're controlling him somehow."

"That's impossible."

"Prove it."

Maren opened her mouth to say something and paused. I could tell by the look in her eyes she was doubting herself.

"Stretch your wings out."

Drakus did as she instructed, unfurling his massive wings. They easily spanned forty feet in length, and the tips had what looked like barbed talons. They differed greatly from the small horns that protruded from Sion's wings.

"You're telling me you don't know how you're controlling him?" I asked.

"I honestly do not know."

The witch has blocked her mind against me, Drakus's voice startled me. *She must be powerful indeed to control me.*

She is formidable with magic, I replied.

Tell her to release me.

Do you think we're fools?

His words confirmed my suspicions, though. Maren was indeed controlling him, but how?

I snorted. "Drakus wants you to release him."

"Even if I knew how, I wouldn't."

Told you.

When I get free, I will flame you both to ash, Drakus hissed.

"He's angry. Whatever you did, don't stop or we're dead."

"I don't know what I did!" Maren snapped. "I saw him about to burn you to death and I yelled the first thing that came to mind. There was no magic behind my words."

I knelt and inspected the floor where she stood, but I didn't see any runes or anything else that might be the source. I peered up at the cave ceiling, but it was too dark to make out anything.

"It must be something in here," I said. "Do you sense any magic?"

"Nothing other than the orbs."

"You brought them?"

"I wasn't going to leave them on the ship for those pirates to take," Maren replied.

"You think they're pirates, too, huh?"

"Of course they are."

I nodded in agreement. "Let me see the orbs."

Maren reached down and loosened her right boot, then fumbled around before straightening back up. She held the three orbs in her hands.

"I thought you said it wasn't safe to touch them?"

"That was before I had time to mess with them. It's safe."

I looked at each one, and I noticed that only two of them swirled with color. The third, the blue one, was a solid color. I flicked my eyes from the orb to Drakus, then to Maren.

"It must be the orb," I said. "There's no other explanation. And it looks different from when we found it."

Maren held the blue orb up so that Drakus could see it.

"Is this what binds you?"

She taunts me, Drakus's voice filled my mind. *She does not allow me to speak to her, yet asks me a question. Where did she get those cursed things?*

Do you know what they are? I asked.

Of course I do, human. They are the cruinne.

What do they do?

You do not know? Drakus growled. *I will not share their secrets with you.*

"The orb must keep him from speaking to you," I said to Maren. "He says those are called cruinne, but he will not explain what that means."

"Tell Eldwin what the cruinne are."

The cruinne are imbued with the souls of dragons, Drakus said. *They were forged to control dragons against their will.*

How many are there? I asked.

Five.

I looked from the dragon to the orbs. Red, blue, green. If two were missing, they must be black and white. An orb for each color.

"The orbs control dragons. Drakus says there are five of them. When we found these, the box had spots for two more, but they were missing. Someone must have found them."

"Maybe," Maren said. "That, or whoever had these was trying to find the other two."

"It had to be someone from your family. The royal crest was plastered all over that place."

"I think you might be right. That would explain the reason the royal dragon riders are separate from the other schools. It must have something to do with control over dragons. Maybe my ancestors were trying to gain control of the Order."

"If that's true, then what your father is doing isn't some crazy plot he came up with on his own. He's trying to execute what your ancestors attempted to do."

"He won't succeed. Not when we have these."

"We need to keep these a secret. If anyone finds out what they can do …"

"Wars will be waged over them," Maren said. "The knowledge of these orbs stays between us."

"What should we do with him?" I asked, nodding at Drakus. "We can't assume he'll stay here and behave himself when we leave."

Maren chewed on her lower lip. "It doesn't seem right to kill him, but I don't know how the magic of these orbs works. If I order him to stay here, how long does that command stick? I have no way of knowing."

I didn't want to kill a dragon either, but it seemed we had little choice in the matter. If we left him alive, he could come after us or turn the other wild dragons on us. It was a risk I didn't like.

"Let me try something," I said, taking the blue orb from her. "Take human form."

Drakus's body shifted and morphed until he appeared as a human. The sapphire jewels on his necklace glinted under the torchlight.

"You will remain as a human and stay confined here until I say otherwise."

"What about food?" Maren asked. "He'll starve to death if he can't leave the cave."

"Fine. You will remain a human and stay within close range of the Whispering Cliffs. You will not travel beyond the waterfall."

The orb vibrated softly in my hand, and Drakus's eyes seemed to glaze over. I gave the orb back to Maren.

"How's that? We don't kill him, but he can't leave."

Maren smiled at me. "Thank you," she silently mouthed.

13

We left the cave through another entrance that was hidden by shadows. It took some time, but Sion and Demris eventually found the other end of it and took us to the top of the cliffs. I wanted to tell Sion about the orbs and the power they held, but the knowledge wasn't safe to share. I locked all thoughts about them behind an impenetrable mental wall.

Did you kill Drakus?

No, I answered. *We were able to convince him to stay put and let us take the others back to Osnen.*

Truly? Sion asked.

Truly.

She nuzzled her snout against my chest. *Tyrval was right to send you here. Now the Order will live on, and we will drive the king's forces back.*

I hope so, I said. *We still have to ask the dragons to come with us.*

They will come. They have lived under a tyrant too long. Freedom gives hope.

We shall see. Can you take me to the cave of the dragon we spoke to? Maren and Demris will wait here.

Yes.

I gave Maren a knowing look, and she subtly nodded. Sion launched into the air, and we flew over the plateau. At the edge of the cliffs, she swooped down and spun in a circle, landing on the ledge of the cave. I dismounted and stepped past Sion, trudging into the darkness. This time, she didn't stop me.

You are alive, the dragon said. *I am surprised.*

Then you will be more surprised to know that Drakus has agreed to let any dragon who wishes to leave to do so.

The glowing eyes of the dragon stared at me, and I felt as if he were searching my soul, that he could somehow detect my lie.

You have done what I thought was impossible. I will go, but my brethren must make their own decision.

Can you gather them together? I will tell them what I told you, and they can decide for themselves what they will do.

My brethren are already gathered in the main cavern. It is feeding time, and Drakus will be there to give us food. Follow me.

The dragon's eyes disappeared from view, and I glanced back at Sion.

Stay here, I said.

Where are you going?

To speak with the other dragons. They must make their choice to stay here or go with us.

I should come with you, she replied. *In case anything happens.*

I'll be fine. As you said, they will see my character and know that coming with us is a good thing.

Sion rumbled, and I could feel her uncertainty in the bond, but she didn't argue. That was good. It would make things easier for me if the dragon chose not to leave.

I'll be back soon. If there's trouble, I'll let you know.

Very well.

I walked blindly further into the cave, keeping my hands outstretched in front of me to ensure I didn't bump into anything. The light from the cave entrance behind me slowly faded, and the darkness was absolute. The sound of the dragon's claws scraping against the stone echoed ahead of me, and I followed the direction of the noise.

A few minutes later, flickering lights appeared. They were spaced along the walls, similar to Drakus's chamber. The blue dragon in front of me led the way into an enormous cavern that was carved out of the interior of the cliffs. I stopped, my eyes widening in disbelief.

Hundreds of dragons were gathered in the cavern. Here and there, their scales glinted from the magical lights. Every color was present except for white. Those dragons preferred the cold, and this tropical place was too humid for them. I reached down and touched the coin pouch at my waist, tracing the outline of the dragon orbs with my finger. If things didn't go according to plan, I would use them to ensure my safety.

At least, that's what I told myself I would do. I wanted to believe that was the only reason I took them, but I knew deep down my ulterior motives were the driving force. The wild dragons were coming back to Osnen whether or not they agreed to. The only problem I foresaw was the black dragons. They were few in number, but they could still cause trouble. I inhaled a deep breath and continued into the cavern. Every dragon eye turned to look at me.

All was silent, but I knew there was likely a chorus of dragon voices as they spoke to one another. They were probably confused, maybe even angry. Considering the lies Drakus had told them, there was no telling what they might be thinking. The blue dragon paused, his head snaking back to look at me.

You may speak when you are ready.

I nodded and looked around the cavern. Despite the power of the orbs at my fingertips, I had many doubts. The magic had been strong enough to control Drakus, but he was a single dragon. What if the magic didn't work against this many? There were easily two or three hundred of the creatures. I pushed the doubts aside. If this failed, then the Citadel would fall and the Order would fade away.

What is your name? I asked.

The dragon was quiet a moment, then said, *Getarros.*

I am Eldwn.

Getarros turned his head to face his brethren. I cleared my throat.

"Greetings! I am Eldwin Baines. I'm sure you are wondering why a human is here in your home, and I assure you I am a friend and an ally. In my land, dragons and humans work together to ensure the realm remains peaceful. We bond with one another, sharing our lives and thoughts. The reason I have come here is simple. Dragons are few, and to continue to live in peace, we need more dragons."

I paused to let the information sink in. Now would be the hard part of trying to undo years of indoctrination within a few minutes. I didn't think the odds of succeeding were good, but I wanted to try convincing them honestly before using the orbs.

"I know what you're thinking. Drakus hates humans and will never agree to let you leave these cliffs. The good news is I have already spoken with Drakus. He has agreed to let you all make your own choice. You can stay here with him, or you can come to the land I come from. Dragons are revered in Osnen, and the people will treat you well."

I stopped talking and looked around the cavern, making eye contact with random dragons. It was impossible to read their expressions, so I did not know what they might be thinking. Getarros turned his head to look at me.

You spoke well, he said.

Thank you. What do they think of my offer?

Some find it difficult to believe that Drakus has agreed to let them leave, but many more are excited to see what the world holds outside of this place.

That was good news, and I felt a small amount of relief.

There are a few whose loyalty to Drakus is deep. They do not believe you, and they refuse to leave.

Let me guess. The black dragons?

How did you know?

I've had a few experiences with some like them. Black dragons can be ... difficult.

I know this well, Getarros said. *Please tell us what needs to be done.*

"If you want to come with me to my land, meet me on the beach. There is a ship there, a vessel made of wood. When all those who want to leave have gathered, I will lead you to Osnen."

The black dragons were small in number, but every one of them left the cavern. I assumed Drakus must have brainwashed them well to garner such devotion.

They are up to something, Getarros said.

14

I stood on the deck of *The Dirty Jewel* and watched as countless dragons left the Whispering Cliffs, taking flight and making their way down to the beach. I was glad I didn't have to use the orbs, but a small, dark part of me was disappointed. As soon as I rejoined Maren, I discreetly passed her the artifacts. The temptation to use such power was great, and I knew I could not trust myself with them. I was confident Maren could see that, and she would keep them safely stored out of my reach.

Getarros was the first to land near the ship. I couldn't sense his emotions since we weren't bonded, but I could see the excitement in his eyes. The hope of being free had awakened something in the dragon, and I was glad to see the vigor in him. Maren had gone below deck to hide the orbs, and Sion and Demris sat near the ship, watching the sky.

You have done a great thing, Sion said. *Hope radiates from them just as the sun shines.*

We can thank Tyrval for that, I replied. *Without her, we would never have known this place existed. I fear that some of them will fall in battle against the king's forces, and that will be my fault for convincing them to come with us.*

Sacrifice is the path to hope. Some of us may perish, but it is for a cause greater than ourselves. Osnen will be a safer place without Erling.

I know, but I am making them trade one tyrant for another.

Not so. They are leaving one tyrant to take down a different one and find a place where they can live in peace. It is a good change.

I had to trust that Sion was right because I didn't want the innocent blood of anyone else on my hands, dragon or human.

"Ne'er thought I'd see anythin' like this afore," Malin said as he stepped beside me.

"Me neither," I replied. "They're beautiful creatures."

"Dangerous, ye mean."

"They can be, but they can also be gentle. They're only dangerous when it's necessary. What do you know about dragons?"

"Not much, me boy. Only what the rumors say in the taverns."

"I put little stock in rumors," I said. "Sure, they may have a kernel of truth to them, but usually, they're just exaggerated claims."

"Aye, that be true in sometimes. Yer dragon ain't done me no wrong, so me ship is always open to ye. I just hope these are as trustworthy."

"I'm sure they are."

Maren came back above deck, and we shared a knowing look. The orbs were safely hidden. She joined us at the helm.

"There are so many," she said.

"Are you surprised?" I asked.

"A little, yes. It usually takes more time and effort to break years of brainwashing, but I suppose dragons are different in that regard."

"Freedom changes people. I'm sure that's true for dragons as well."

"What are ye talkin' about?" Malin asked. "Ye speak like these beasts were prisoners."

"They were," I replied. "We freed them from the tyrant that kept them here."

Malin lowered his voice. "Did ye kill 'im?"

I quickly shook my head. "No, we didn't have to. Let's just say I persuaded him into his own prison."

"So he might stir up trouble, then, aye?"

"Anything is possible, but I don't think we have to worry about him. His army of slaves is now free, and they will not go back to serving him without a fight. Besides that, most of the dragons have chosen to come to Osnen. He doesn't have many that are willingly loyal to him."

"I don't know about dragons, but losing power can drive men to do dark things," Malin said, frowning.

"Were you able to replace the rudder?" I asked, changing the subject. I didn't want him to focus on the negative. To be honest, I didn't want to think about what Drakus would do if he somehow escaped.

"Aye, it be fixed. The *Jewel* should sail just fine. Yer dragons will have to lift 'er up and take 'er past the current."

"That won't be a problem," I said. "I was thinking we could fly back. My dragon seems to have restored her strength, so we won't need to bother you with sailing us back to Osnen."

"Ye paid me for a job, me boy. It ain't no bother on me. If ye want to fly, that not be a problem, but I'd enjoy yer company if ye wanted to sail."

"We haven't made up our minds just yet," Maren chimed in. "Eldwin and I will discuss it further and let you know before we depart."

"Speaking of, do you think it's wise to lead these dragons in the dark?" I asked Maren. "It'll be dark soon. Maybe we should camp here for the night and set out in the morning."

"I think that's a good idea," Maren said. "As long as the captain doesn't have any objections?"

"None," Malin answered.

I nodded. "Then it's decided. We'll camp here tonight and leave at dawn."

"I'll let the crew know. They be itching to get back on the sea, as I am, but it be wise to travel with plenty o' daylight."

Malin strode off, and Maren waited until he was out of sight to speak.

"I don't think we should leave him behind.

What if he comes back here looking for something?"

"There's no treasure to be found," I replied.

"Not that we know of, but that's not the point. He's a pirate, Eldwin. He may turn the ship around once we're gone and come back just to check."

"That would be foolish. He knows wards are protecting this place. And this ship wouldn't survive the impact of falling from that." I looked toward the massive waterfall that thundered in the distance.

"Maybe I'm being paranoid," Maren admitted. "Still, I think we should sail on the ship. Demris and Sion could take the lead and guide the wild dragons to the Citadel. They would arrive faster and be able to help Anesko."

"I don't like the idea of being without our dragons, but I do like the latter part of your plan. That would certainly bolster the Citadel's defenses. I'll go speak with Getarros now and let him know what we've discussed."

I departed the ship and walked along the beach to where the blue dragon was basking. He turned his attention to me as I approached.

I wanted to let you know our plan. I'm not troubling you, am I?

Speak freely, Getarros said. *I'm enjoying the sunlight.*

I smiled. *Good. I'm glad to see that. It will be dusk soon, so we are going to camp here for the night. We'll leave when the sun rises so that we have plenty of daylight. Since none of you have ever left the cliffs, I don't want to lose anyone in the dark. I know dragons can see perfectly at night, but if there's a storm or any other problem, I'd rather be on the safe side.*

I see the wisdom in that.

Excellent. There's one other thing. If my dragon were to lead you to our land while I stay behind on the ship, would you follow her?

Getarros blinked and drew his head back. *You have liberated us from our god. We will follow you and do as you ask, but we will not follow your dragon without you. We have a healthy distrust of one another, and your dragon is unknown to us. I'm sure you understand.*

Yes, of course. That's why I wanted to ask you before deciding. I appreciate your honesty.

I appreciate your respect.

Likewise, I said. *We will travel together, then. Please let your brethren know to eat their fill before morning. It will be a long while before you have something to eat besides fish.*

We will be ready.

I nodded, smiling again. *Very good.*

Turning, I headed back to the ship and let Maren know the wild dragons would not go on ahead of us.

"That's frustrating, but I understand his logic. It's a miracle they are willing to follow us at all, so we should be happy about that."

"I agree."

We spent the rest of the evening relaxing on the deck of the *Jewel* as Malin told stories of his adventures on the sea. The dragons took turns hunting for food among the jungle that stretched across the island surrounding the cliffs, and Sion joined a few of the groups, offering advice on how to stalk prey.

It was a rare moment of peacefulness, but in the back of my mind, I knew it wouldn't last. We were about to go to war with the king, and it was going to be bloody. Many would die, dragons and humans, and despite the army of dragons we'd gathered, victory wasn't guaranteed. I tried my best to enjoy the peace while we had it.

After dinner had been served and the moon was high overhead, we turned in for the night. I laid beside Maren, my arm draped over her, and I was just dozing off when I heard something. I opened my eyes and stared at the ceiling, listening intently. What was that? A moment later, a tremor shook the ship. I bolted upright, as did Maren.

"What's going on?" she asked.

Before I could say anything, Sion's voice entered my mind with an answer.

We're being attacked!

15

I scrambled out of bed and hurriedly put my boots on, then grabbed my sword and rushed above deck. Maren followed quickly behind me, and I saw members of the ship's crew sprinting to the starboard railing. The night sky above was clear, and the moonlight revealed a multitude of dark silhouettes battling overhead.

Roars of both anger and pain resounded, pushing away my drowsiness, and the flames of their breath bathed the *Jewel* in an orange glow. The black dragons from earlier were the aggressors. Getarros had been right about them. I glanced at the cliffs. There was no doubt Drakus was behind this.

"What do they hope to accomplish?" I asked, turning my gaze to Maren. "They are vastly outnumbered."

"Drakus knows what we have," she replied. "I'll bet he sent them here to destroy them."

"We need to protect them. Where are they?"

"I'll get them," Maren said. She only managed a few steps before a torrent of flame spilled onto the deck from above, catching the *Jewel* on fire. I pulled Maren away from the heat and pushed her toward the gangplank.

"Off the ship!" I shouted.

"We need the orbs!"

She was right, but it was more than that. I *wanted* them, and the power they held. It was almost painful leaving them behind, but perhaps that wasn't a bad thing. Maren and I hit the beach running. I scanned the area for Sion, but I didn't see her.

Where are you?

Fighting, she replied. *Take shelter somewhere!*

I glanced back at the *Jewel*. The fire was spreading quickly along the timber, and the crew was abandoning the ship. I didn't see Malin among them, and I feared he was trapped below deck. I skidded to a halt.

"Find somewhere safe!" I shouted at Maren. "I'll be back!"

I dashed toward the ship before she could argue or question me and ran up the gangplank. The heat was suffocating. I watched the flames race up the masts, burning the ropes and sails with impossible speed and fury.

"Get off the ship, me boy!"

Malin was at the helm, his right arm shielding his face. I sprinted across the deck to where he was.

"Come on!"

"A cap'n goes down with 'is ship," he said, his left hand keeping a tight grip on the wheel.

"That's insane," I replied. "There's no reason for you to die here. Please, come with me."

Malin shook his head. "No, me boy. Me time

has come. Ye get off while ye can. That lass out there needs ye."

I clenched my right hand into a fist, ready to knock him out and carry him to safety if I had to, but a dragon glided overhead and breathed more fire onto the ship, forcing me to retreat.

"Go, boy!"

I didn't want to leave Malin, but there was nothing I could do now. He'd made his decision, but he wouldn't have been in danger at all if it weren't for me. Yet again, innocent blood was on my hands. I cursed and fled the ship. Midway up the beach, an explosion roared behind me.

A gaping hole was open where the cargo was held, and the ship was fully ablaze now. Perhaps the orbs would survive the fire, and when the flames died, we could retrieve them. That thought was dashed when two black dragons dropped from the sky and grabbed onto the flaming ship with their rear legs. They flapped their wings and lifted it from the sand just high enough to toss the vessel into the water.

The ship quickly disappeared below the surface, and any hope of getting the orbs back died a watery death. An unearthly roar drowned out all the other noise, and I looked in the sound's direction. A massive shadow departed from the cliffs, winging its way toward the beach.

Drakus was free. The orbs had been destroyed.

He flew over the beach, flaming and snapping at

dragons as he whipped past. He was enormous, easily three times the size of Demris, and his body blotted out the moon when he flew overhead. I ran for the jungle, heading in the direction I'd seen Maren go. I found her waiting amid some thick brush.

"Are you all right?" she asked.

"Yes. I tried to get Malin, but …" I shook my head. "He wouldn't leave the ship. The orbs are gone, and Drakus is free."

"I saw. We need to stop him."

"How? He's massive. We don't stand a chance."

"The other dragons will need to band together to defeat him. I can use my magic to help, but it will take our combined efforts."

Rally the wild dragons to take down Drakus, I told Sion. *Maren will aid you.*

I'm already ahead of you, she replied. *What does she have in mind?*

"What are you going to do?" I asked Maren.

"I can bind him, but I'll need to be directly below him. If they can keep him still long enough for me to speak the words, he'll be at their mercy."

Get him over the jungle. Maren will do the rest.

We'll do our best. Be ready.

It had been a long time since I'd felt useless, and I didn't like it. Without magic, I could do nothing but wait and watch the unfolding carnage.

Drakus and his black dragons were tearing a path of destruction along the beach. They were outnumbered, but those who had chosen to leave had clearly never been in a battle before. They scattered in fear, trying to escape.

Sion and Demris joined the fray, along with Getarros and a few brave dragons. They roared in challenge, rallying their fleeing brethren. Drakus's minions turned their wrath on them.

Be careful, I bade Sion. *Drakus is a mighty foe.*

He is big like the Assembly members, but he is not invincible. His bulk slows him down. It will be easy to avoid his attacks.

Sion sounded confident, but I was still worried about her. She roared and barrel rolled between two black dragons, coming out behind them and raking her rear claws along their haunches. Demris went head-to-head with his own foe, easily dominating the smaller creature. Getarros held back, and at first, I thought he was second-guessing himself with Drakus in sight. A host of black dragons ringed the behemoth, but when one of them wasn't paying attention, Getarros charged ahead, snapping his jaws around the dragon's neck.

He jerked his head from side to side, much like a dog holding a snake, and a sickening crack rang out. I blanched as the black dragon went lifeless and fell to the beach with a crash. The dragons who had rallied to Sion and Demris's call followed Getarros's example and launched an attack on the other dragons guarding Drakus. Snapping jaws and swiping claws were everywhere, and in the darkness, it was hard to tell who was winning.

Emboldened by their stand against the tyrant, more dragons winged their way to the battle. Drakus's minions fell before their ferocity. As the sky filled with dragons, Drakus's confidence faltered. I watched as he retreated, and Sion and Demris guided the horde of creatures onward, herding Drakus toward the jungle.

"Get ready," I said, looking over my shoulder. "They're bringing him this way."

Maren nodded and looked to the sky, lifting her arms. The dragons pushed Drakus further and further, and once he crossed over the jungle's canopy, Maren began her spell. Ethereal tendrils sprouted from her palms and began zig-zagging their way up, higher and higher. When Drakus was overhead, his shadow smothered everything in darkness. The tendrils glowed with a faint white light, creating an eerie atmosphere among the trees.

He's going to flee, Sion said.

No, he's not. Maren won't let him.

As if reading my mind, Maren stretched her arms straight up. The tendrils raced through the leafy canopy and began encircling around Drakus. He roared in surprise but could not fight her magic. The tendrils bound him in place.

Let Getarros decide his fate, I said.

There was a moment of calm. And then the host of dragons converged on Drakus, biting and clawing him until his giant form slumped in death. Maren slowly came to stand beside me, her spell still intact.

"Guide me," she whispered.

I rested a hand on her back and led her out of the jungle and onto the beach. Once we were clear of the danger, she released the magic and Drakus's body crashed down among the trees, leaving a wake of devastation.

With a suddenness that surprised me, Getarros zipped down from the sky, landing on the beach. He charged toward us, snarling.

You lied to us! He growled fiercely.

Despite all the time I had spent around dragons, his rage frightened me. I swallowed hard and fell to my knees before him, humbling myself. Sion landed nearby, growling a warning at Getarros.

Do not attack him, I told her, then I turned my mind toward him.

Forgive me, Getarros. I did lie to you, to all of you. I thought I was doing what was best to ensure you and your brethren were free from Drakus's yoke. I did not want to deceive you, but I knew Drakus would not let you leave of your own volition.

Did you also lie about your land? Did we trade one master for another?

That was the only thing I said that was false, I replied. *Everything else was true.*

Getarros towered over me, his chest heaving with heavy breaths. I didn't know if he believed me, or if he would still come with us to Osnen. I couldn't blame him. Although my intentions were just, my methods had been dishonest.

I will forgive you, but you will need to earn my trust once more. That will not be a simple task.

I will do whatever it takes to prove myself to you.

We shall see.

Getarros trudged away, leaving claw marks in the sand. Maren laid a hand on my shoulder comfortingly.

"That could have gone worse," she said.

"It also could have gone better. I shouldn't have lied to them. It wasn't right."

"I know. And I'm glad you realize that. Will they still come with us?"

"Yes."

"Then all is not lost. We can still save the Citadel. We will regroup and rest, and tomorrow we make the journey home as we planned."

I rose to my feet and embraced Maren. My eyes roamed the shore. The bodies of dragons littered the area, and I spotted a few of the crew members from *The Dirty Jewel* among them.

We had won a battle here, but a war awaited us in Osnen, and this was only a glimpse of the potential devastation that was coming. I hugged

Maren tighter and prayed I wouldn't lose her or Sion to the coming darkness.

THE END OF BOOK 13

ABOUT THE AUTHOR

Richard Fierce is a fantasy and space opera author. He's been writing since childhood, but began publishing in 2007. Since then, he's written multiple novels and short stories.

In 2000, Richard won Poet of the Year for his poem *The Darkness*. He's also one of the creative brains behind the Allatoona Book Festival, a literary event in Acworth, Georgia.

A recovering retail worker, he now works in the tech industry when he's not busy writing.

He's married and has three step-daughters (pray for him), three dogs (huskies!), a cat, and two ferrets. He basically has a zoo.

His love affair with fantasy was born in high school when a friend's mother gave him a copy of *Dragons of Spring Dawning* by Margaret Weis and Tracy Hickman.